# COAST GUARD TO THE RESCUE

By Ace Landers
Illustrated by Kenny Kiernan

SCHOLASTIC INC.

All rights reserved. Published by Scholastic Inc., *Publishers since 1920*. SCHOLASTIC and associated logos are trademarks and/or registered trademarks of Scholastic Inc.

The publisher does not have any control over and does not assume any responsibility for author or third-party websites or their content.

No part of this publication may be reproduced, stored in a retrieval system, or transmitted in any form or by any means, electronic, mechanical, photocopying, recording, or otherwise, without written permission of the publisher. For information regarding permission, write to Scholastic Inc., Attention: Permissions Department, 557 Broadway, New York, NY 10012.

ISBN 978-1-338-21022-4

10 9 8 7 6 5 4 3          18 19 20 21 22

Printed in the U.S.A.   40

First printing 2018

Book design by Angela Jun

"Good morning, LEGO City, and thanks for tuning in to today's weather report! We've got a beautiful day ahead of us: sunny with a chance of WOW! So don't waste the day staying inside. It's time for some fun in the sun!"

No one in LEGO® City ever misses the morning weather report. Everyone is ready for a bright and perfect day.

A surfer dude heads out to catch some waves. Jet Skiers are totally ready to race across the water. A scuba diver can't wait to explore under the sea.

"And we're clear," says the camerawoman. "Great job, everyone!"

With the weather report over, the weatherman decides to enjoy the day, too. He's going to take his brand-new sailboat, *Sunny Side Up*, out for a ride.

With so many people visiting the water, the LEGO City coast guard is on patrol. The coast guard's job is to make sure everyone has a safe and fun day.

The warm weather is so peaceful that no one is in danger—so even the coast guard crew has time for a little rest and relaxation.

A little fishing, a little game of Go Fish, and a little yoga make the crew healthy, stealthy, and wise.

But then there is something strange on the horizon. Gray storm clouds start rolling in fast. The waves in the water become choppy.

The captain realizes that the storm is too big for one ship to handle the rescue on its own. It is time to call for reinforcements.

There is a rumble in the sky. It's a coast guard airplane swooping in! It will save the surfer before the strong tide pulls him into the open water.

"Dude, am I ever so pumped to see you!" cheers the surfer. "These waves are too gnarly to hang ten!"

Farther out, a coast guard helicopter spots the scuba diver. A rescue diver is lowered into the water on a hook to save the diver.

"This must be what a fish feels like!" says the scuba diver. "You caught me hook, line, and sinker!"

There is still someone else who needs the coast guard's help. It's the weatherman!

He tries to control his sailboat as it rocks back and forth in the wind. But he has bigger problems as he looks out at the ocean. "Oh, no. It appears to be cloudy with a 100 percent chance of . . . SHARKS!"

The weatherman finds a flare and fires it into the sky. A bright burst of light tells the coast guard exactly where he is.

Suddenly, the shark swims alongside the sailboat. The shark pushes it carefully through the waves toward a small island! "Whoa! You don't want to eat me. You want to save me!" the weatherman exclaims.

Once they reach the island, the weatherman leaps from the boat and waves to the shark.

"That was a fin-tastic rescue!" yells the weatherman as the shark swims back into the ocean.

The coast guard helicopter lands on the island to pick up the stranded weatherman. One of the rescuers says, "We're glad you're okay, sir. But what happened to your weather prediction?"

Suddenly, the rain clears, the water calms down, and the sun starts to peek through the clouds.

The weatherman shrugs and smiles. "I said it would be sunny today. I just didn't say *how much* of the day would be sunny."

Luckily for LEGO City, the coast guard is always ready to protect and serve—even on the sunniest days.